PHONICS

Get Up, Tim!

Practising CVC words with short vowel sounds

First published in 2007 by
Franklin Watts
338 Euston Road
London
NW1 3BH

Franklin Watts Australia
Hachette Children's Books
Level 17/207 Kent Street
Sydney
NSW 2000

A CIP catalogue record for this book is available
from the British Library.

ISBN: 978 0 7496 7121 1 (hbk)
ISBN: 978 0 7496 7308 6 (pbk)

Series Editor: Jackie Hamley
Series Advisors: Dr Barrie Wade, Dr Hilary Minns
Series Designer: Peter Scoulding

Printed in China

Franklin Watts is a division of
Hachette Children's Books.

READING CORNER

PHONICS

Get Up, Tim!

by
Sue Graves

Illustrated by
Melanie Sharp

W
FRANKLIN WATTS
LONDON•SYDNEY

Sue Graves
"My children are hopeless at getting up, too. Perhaps I should shoot water at them!"

Melanie Sharp
"Waking my boys up in the mornings is always full of fun and games!"

"Get up, Tim!"

6

"Not yet, Dad!"
Tim did not get up.

"Get up, Tim!"

"Not yet, Dad!"

9

11

Tim did not get up.

15

"Yes, Dad!"

But Tim did not get up.

Dad had fun.

Tim got wet.

Tim got up!